USA TODAY BESTSELLING AUTHOR

SUSAN STEPHENS

Editor: Linda Ingmanson

ISBN

ePub: 978-1-910604-64-9

Mobi: 978-1-910604-66-3

Print: 978-1-910604-67-0

This is a work of fiction. Names, characters, places and incidents are either the product of the author's imagination or used fictitiously. Any resemblance to actual persons, living or dead, businesses, companies, or events is entirely coincidental.

DEDICATION

To my readers — thank you for embracing my fierce heroes and the equally fierce women who bring them to their knees. Your support means more than you know.

With gratitude to Glass Slipper WebDesign for my brilliant cover, and to Linda and Toni for their meticulous editing and copy editing. Your talent makes these stories shine.

Finally, to my family — thank you for your patience while I disappear into my world of danger, devotion, and hard-won happy ever afters. I couldn't do this without you.

AUTHOR'S NOTE

Elijah was never meant to be easy.

He's controlled, guarded, a man who survives by locking everything down until the one woman who truly sees him walks back into his life. Writing his story meant peeling back layers of strength to reveal vulnerability, and reminding myself that even the toughest heroes have breaking points.

Sable doesn't stand behind him. She stands with him. Always.

I loved writing the secondary characters because they provided the quiet heartbeat of this story, proving that love, loyalty, and shared history are worth fighting for.

To those of you who have been waiting for Elijah, thank you. Your loyalty, messages, and passion for my Blood and Thunder series mean more than I can say.

Elijah

A Blood and Thunder novel

Camo paint cut harsh lines across his face, emphasizing the brutal planes. He wore dark tactical gear: combat trousers, scuffed boots, a fitted black shirt with the sleeves shoved to his elbows, every inch of him thick with muscle, dust, and dangerous intent. A suppressed carbine rode his shoulder; spare mags loaded his vest; the pistol strapped to his thigh and the knife across his chest completed the impression of a man carved for war.

He was not a reassuring sight.

Elijah had never tried to be.

PROLOGUE

A small island off Malta in the Mediterranean Sea

A single naked bulb buzzed overhead, its weak glow trembling across cellar walls slick with damp and rot. Shadows clung to the huddle of filthy, skeletal shapes pressed together as if the touch of another living human could fend off despair. The stench of fear, sweat, and excrement hung in the air like something alive.

A key scraped in the lock.

Chains rattled when mothers dragged children behind them. The captives drew inward as the door exploded open.

Elijah Steel filled the threshold.

Camo paint cut harsh lines across his face emphasizing the brutal planes. He wore dark tactical gear: combat trousers, scuffed boots, a fitted black shirt with the sleeves shoved to his elbows, every inch of him thick with muscle, dust, and dangerous intent. A suppressed carbine rode his shoulder; spare mags loaded his vest; the pistol strapped to his thigh and the knife across his chest completed the impression of a man carved for war.

He was not a reassuring sight.

Elijah had never tried to be.

Sable Alexandrovna stepped in beside him, equally armed, equally lethal. Their eyes swept the room with cold appraisal. Two predators assessing prey and threat with the same detached precision.

The first guard made barely a sound. Elijah struck fast, snapping the man's neck with a single brutal twist. Beside him, Sable's blade flashed, and the second guard hit the concrete, blood gushing.

Gunfire erupted. The prisoners shielded their faces as shards of concrete shot into the air. A machete swung toward them—too slow. Elijah hurled Sable out of its path and met the attacker head-on, ending the threat with merciless efficiency.

Blood and Thunder team members flooded in behind them, herding captives toward the exit. Amid the chaos, Elijah and Sable found themselves pressed close—shoulder to shoulder, breath mingling, adrenaline sharpening everything between them. Sable's lips tilted the slightest fraction in wordless acceptance of a bond neither could kill.

Two shadows moving as one, they snatched keys from the dead guards' belts.

"You're free," Sable told the prisoners, her voice low and controlled, as she worked the locks.

A small girl flung her arms around her neck. Sable froze for a heartbeat, then gently pried the child loose. "You're safe now," she murmured, her eyes scanning for threats.

"On your feet," Elijah ordered a dazed youth. "We need help. Name?"

"Ivor."

"Some of your people can't walk."

"I'll carry them," the boy answered fiercely as boots thundered down the stairwell above.

"If you do exactly as we say, you'll make it out alive," Sable told the captives, ushering them toward a trapdoor carved into the floor by one of the team's specialists.

Leading them into the darkness, she paused to watch Elijah wrench the shattered door from its hinges and brace it across the entrance.

Dust sifted down like ash as they crowded the tunnel. Muffled gunfire cracked above, making the rescued shrink in terror until Elijah dropped through the opening, when there was a group sigh of relief. Slamming the trapdoor shut behind him, he roared, "Move! Don't look back!"

It took the slavers less than sixty seconds to breach the barricade. The roof of the tunnel trembled with gunfire and shouted curses. The air filled with grime after each round of fire. This dimmed the torchlight to a flickering glow as Sable pushed the ragged band deeper into the passageway.

"I'll cover you," Elijah called out. "Keep going."

She needed no encouragement. Survival was the only goal as fire and thunder filled the route.

Bursting into the night, she sucked greedily on clean air. The stench of hot metal had burned her lungs, and this welcome change was a reminder she was still alive.

That was something.

She turned back to caring for the prisoners with the confidence of knowing that somewhere behind them, guarding their backs, was Elijah.

He was their avenging angel.

CHAPTER ONE

Seven years later
Grand Harbour Malta

Late-afternoon sun bled across the Mediterranean as Elijah Steel leaned over the rail of his superyacht, the *Seraphim*. Beyond the marina, the ancient walls of Valletta rose in golden splendor, silent and implacable, a reminder of everything the small island had given him.

As well as the things it had taken.

He shouldn't have come back. Yet he had. All because of Sable Alexandrovna No one else could lure him halfway across the world.

Who wouldn't answer the call of a woman supposedly dead?

Woman? She'd been his partner, lover, and his most trusted colleague. Now he wasn't even sure she'd show.

If Sable had returned from the dead, he wasn't sure what he felt. Fury? Hope?

Hope of what? Any chance of reigniting their relationship was as dead as she was supposed to be.

Suspicion, then.

There was plenty of that.

Trust was a rare commodity for him. Sable had once been the exception. Until she vanished without a word.

If she was back, it had to be one hell of a mission she had in mind. In the world of undercover warfare, no one could match his firepower. That could be the only reason she'd decided to come back.

Money, power, success. He had it all. His yacht dominated the harbor. Eighty-five meters of sleek supertech that made other vessels look like outdated toys bobbing in its wake.

He'd built his wealth on military technology so advanced that governments across the world bent to acquire it. Contracts that came his way carried more zeros and more danger than any other team could handle. Only Blood and Thunder had the men, the leadership, the sheer willpower and ability to keep evil at bay.

Which was why, when he was invited to join their elite mercenary family, hidden beneath the facade of an international polo team, he hadn't hesitated. Their moral code appealed to him the way Sable once had.

Success? Yes. Professional satisfaction? Definitely. But something was missing.

He craved action and danger as other men craved a safe, comfortable life, but sometimes late at night, he missed the laughter, the softness—and, okay, the great sex—that had vanished with the woman he was supposed to meet today.

"Sir." His steward's voice snapped him back to the moment. "This came through the private satellite line. Same icon. Several repeats."

"Thank you." Elijah took the encrypted handset and went still as he read the message. Only one individual signed off with the icon of a predator with bared fangs. Not some cute emoji, but a warning, a promise, a brand: the face of a black panther, sleek, silent, controlled violence, wrapped in an elegant package.

Sable's brand.

His lover. His partner. His ghost. *You owe me. Come to Valletta.*

Who else could bait him across the Mediterranean with six words and resurrect every emotion he'd successfully buried with a single digital ghost?

Sable had disappeared off the face of the earth seven years ago. Recently, she'd been officially declared dead. No one was surprised. She had always run into the fire instead of around it. He'd never stopped looking for her. Now he faced the possibility that she had clawed her way back from the grave.

He curled his fist around cold metal hanging beneath his shirt. If she was alive, why had she chosen to stay gone, leaving him with a gold ring on a chain? A wedding band without a bride. A promise turned into a weapon. And now this message from the grave.

Returning to his stateroom, he poured a scotch large enough to make the burn hit hard.

Not hard enough. The possibility that Sable was nearby made his senses scream with awareness. There was nothing he wanted more than to drag her close and demand the truth she owed him.

The thought of touching her again—

A knock on the door forced him to refocus. "Come."

His steward entered, offering a handset.

"Another message, sir."

Noon tomorrow. Our usual place.

Anger gripped him. She was alive and had the audacity to come to him for help.

Breathing steadily, he achieved battlefield calm, the type that led either to violence or to salvation.

Sable tugged the brim of her baseball cap lower as St. Paul's Cathedral tolled noon. The sun was a spotlight on her face, and she couldn't risk being spotted by snitches for slavers.

The sound of sonorous bells rolled down the narrow limestone street, vibrating through her bones like the echo of a memory.

That memory was always Elijah.

She did her best to forget him as she blended into the crowd, but they'd lived here, loved here—at least, she had.

Focus! Risk was ever present for an undercover agent. Safety in numbers? Not here. Not anywhere. The street might be crowded, but who knew what the scrum concealed? There was no such thing as a sanctuary for someone in Sable's line of work, except maybe briefly, when Elijah had been at her side.

Elijah.

Seven years since she'd vanished to save his life, faking her death to sever Black Meridian's hold over her partner. Seven years of ghosts and grit, rebuilding her life in the shadows. Contacting him again for this mission, begging for resources to dismantle the slavers' ring, cracked open the vault she'd buried herself in, leaving her vulnerable to enemies, life, and to Elijah.

Dreams came hot and relentless every night, dragging her under the way his hands used to drag her hips back against him. Last night's frenzied recollection had been the worst. She'd woken, sweat slick and aching, thighs clenched around nothing but memory.

In the dream, Elijah had her pinned to a rain-lashed warehouse wall during that final op, his mouth brutal on her throat, teeth marking skin while his fingers shoved her jeans down just enough. "You think you can walk away from this?" he'd snarled, his voice cold as steel even as he thrust into her hard enough to rattle her teeth.

Hot sex, cold heart was a perfect description of Elijah.

In her dreams, he was merciless, driving deep inside her as she shattered around him. Afterward, his storm-gray eyes locked on hers with calculation. Never a whisper of the softness she'd craved. When a careless tear leaked from her eyes, he barked, "Get your head in the game, Sable. This isn't a fairy tale."

Guilt clawed at her gut as she remembered leaving him cold, without a single word of explanation. Fists clenched, she yelled silently at herself again as she hurried on down the street. Victims of the slavers needed her to be on her game, not softened by lust for a man who held the key to their freedom.

One girl in particular had driven this mission. Anna Marie was in terrible danger. Barely eighteen, she had been lured from home like so many others on the pretext of a lucrative job. They'd met on a quiet island off Malta, where Sable had retreated after shattering Elijah's world. Although working as a cleaner during the day, Anna was already in the slavers' clutches and would be sold on before being transported to who knew where.

How many innocent victims would vanish along with Anna? The pattern was clear: captives herded in silent processions toward a transport that ferried them straight to hell.

Only Elijah could free them with his floating battleship and team of hardened mercenaries.

But this mission could cost him his life.

Her mouth dried at the thought, but then she remembered the prisoners and Anna's pale, distraught face and knew she was right to be here, because Elijah was the best. She had no option but to call on him for help.

When it came to persuading him to overlook the past and help, she held a trump card. There was a woman he'd be desperate to save. She only knew this from an old photograph he carried around. Both Elijah and the woman Mara had been fostered by the same family, and Mara had saved him from a violent home.

Black Meridian did nothing by chance. They shipped assets around the world. Sometimes, a straightforward sale was arranged, but if a prisoner could be used to bring a target out of the shadows, they wouldn't hesitate. It was Mara's bad fortune to be captured. That was how Sable saw her image on the dark web. Elijah was the target; Mara was the lure, making Sable's seven-year separation from him futile.

Far from angering her, it made her all the more determined to rescue the prisoners and obliterate at least one tentacle of Black Meridian.

The imminent meeting with Elijah filled her with dread and excitement. Weaving through the crowd sharpened her senses as she waited for that shift in the air that would tell her he was close. She might not see him right away, but she'd feel him watching from the shadows. Elijah, the ultimate undercover operative, was educated, lethal, and breathtakingly compelling, a force of nature wrapped in self-control.

She was also good at blending into the background. Jogging down stone steps to the seafront, she looked like just another tourist in cut-offs and a vest—if tourists hid blades in their shoes, carried mace in their pockets, and were skilled in Krav Maga.

Ilya Korsakov's training had turned her into a human weapon. The retired KGB operative had seen something in Sable when she was a child in a state orphanage he visited. His methods were brutal but effective. They'd kept her alive more times than she could count.

Crossing the road, she tensed as a scooter roared past too close for comfort, but it was just a delivery driver. Then a ripple gripped her spine, sharp, electric, familiar.

Seven years vanished as if they'd never been apart. Her body knew Elijah, though she couldn't see him yet. Scanning the street revealed nothing. He'd been a shadow since the first day they met.

Except in bed.

A faint smile tugged at her lips, while inwardly she was rejoicing. He had accepted her invitation to meet. The subtle shift in her world proved it.

And he was closing in fast.

Excitement rippled through her as she headed down the final flight of steps. She was heading for a small, shabby café that had been their local when they lived in Valetta. The owners, Frank and Lino, never asked questions. They understood boundaries. Or, perhaps they sensed danger surrounding their two regulars.

Rasping her thumb against a small pebble in her pocket, she thought back to the last time she'd visited the café with Elijah. Amethyst, he'd said as he handed her the stone. "I'll have it polished for you one day."

That was the most emotion he'd ever shown. On a personal note, it was huge. "I don't need a ring," she'd said, "you're enough." Which had been Elijah's cue to shrug and get up to pay the bill, his expression unreadable, but closer to negative than positive.

She pushed the memory aside. What good would it do her? She had no idea what reception she'd get from him today. That damn pebble should have been tossed into the sea years ago.

So why am I closing my fingers around it as if it were a talisman?

CHAPTER TWO

Sable was alive.

He'd spent the past seven years wondering. No body, no proof, was his maxim. During those seven years, he'd grown colder and saw the world without illusion.

But now she was back.

Seeing her had cracked his armor right down the middle. She looked better than the ghost he'd carried around, stronger, sharper, and as appealing as ever. Everything else faded into static.

Almost everything.

A part of him would always remain alert to danger. Habit. Survival. His nature was cast in stone.

The café hadn't changed. Same dented tin chairs, same sun-bleached awning shading scrubbed tables that had witnessed a dozen whispered ops. Tourists drifted past in the shimmering heat, unaware of what was being discussed, while locals lingered over cigarettes and gelato, unconcerned.

No one interacted, which suited two covert operatives.

Sable sat tucked away in a corner, a coffee in one hand, her cell in the other. A stranger might think her relaxed. He knew better. The tilt of her shoulders telegraphed tension. The way she angled the camera on her phone told him she was mapping the scene, searching for him.

Seven years of pent-up frustration flared. Did she think so little of him that it cost her nothing to vanish?

The delicate line of her jaw and the stubborn set of her mouth taunted him. The feel of her body beneath his hands—

He should have moved on. Why couldn't he?

Sable's relentless war against traffickers was the one thing in her favor. Nothing deterred her. She would always throw herself between predator and prey.

That was the only reason he was here. But seeing her again was like a jagged blade rasping over old scars. Her messages had been a shock. Seeing her was worse. Yes, he was relieved that she wasn't in her grave but he couldn't forget she had chosen to be dead to him.

Frank, one of the café's owners, recognized him and wisely pretended otherwise. A flicker of awareness in Sable's eyes told him she'd noticed the shift in Frank's expression and knew he was close by.

Correct.

And he wanted answers.

Poised for action, she lifted her chin, scanning her surroundings without seeming to take interest in anything. Her pulse thundered in her ears. She sensed Elijah as a pressure drop before a storm. He moved like smoke, silent, invisible, lethal. If he wanted to be seen, she'd see him.

Lino broke the tension by approaching with the bill. "Church is the only cool place today," he said, glancing toward the Anglican cathedral across the street.

"Thanks for the advice." She slid cash across the table, steadying her breathing. Lino's comment wasn't a throw-away, but a direction.

Dodging tourists and traffic, she crossed the road and entered the cathedral. Hefty stone walls swallowed sound, and light fell in slanting halos across the stripped-back interior. It was blissfully cool. If she'd got it wrong and Lino wasn't dropping a huge hint, at least she'd have a chance to grab a few moments of tran-quility.

He watched her slide into a pew, head bowed as though in prayer. To an outsider, she was a woman seeking peace, but he knew the camera on her cell was reversed, showing every-thing behind her. She would have noted the nearest exit the second she stepped inside.

He waited to be sure they were alone, then moved.

She sensed him before the camera did its work. Turning, she stared up at him. Their eyes locked. His senses sharpened, hunter keen. Observing Sable from a distance had been manageable. Seeing her without a shadow or barrier between them was something else.

"Sable." He kept his voice low, emotion buried deep.

"Elijah."

His name on her tongue was like long-forgotten music, but sentimentality had no place.

"Thank you for coming. I didn't see you until you were right behind me. Of course," she added, "you're too good for that."

"No slouch yourself," he said, giving her cell a pointed glance. "So, why did you bring me here?"

She blinked at his cold tone, but showed no other emotion. "It's always the slavers. You must have known…"

He didn't answer.

"I wouldn't have contacted you unless I was desperate," she went on.

"Desperate and dead?"

"I recovered."

"So, it seems." He let a beat pass. "I don't have time to waste, Sable."

"Will you sit? Just for a moment?"

"Here? Too public. Prayers won't save me—or you."

Her voice thinned with urgency. "There's no one else I can turn to. Lives are at stake, and this is time critical. Only you and the Blood and Thunder team can shut down this latest band of monsters."

"I never deploy the team unless the intel is flawless."

"It is," she assured him, her gaze steady. "This band of people traffickers is bigger, stronger, and better organized than anything we've seen before. I have to do something. We must."

"We?"

"I can guess what you think of me, but this isn't about us. Please think about the captives and the hell they're going through. If there's even the slimmest chance we can save them—"

"Go on."

"A cleaner in my building raised my suspicions. Anna Marie was too young and too scared to be on her own. When I saw men in a black SUV collecting her, I grew suspicious."

"So you followed them?"

"It was worth the risk."

His jaw tightened. She knew the rule: never approach hostiles alone.

"I followed them to a derelict house and waited outside. Anna Marie eventually emerged. Dragged out by two thugs, she was dressed like a doll, a very frightened doll. They pushed her into the back of an SUV and drove off. The next day, when she was back cleaning in my building, I approached her. She broke down, and told me there were dozens like her—girls, boys, older prisoners. Held in filth. No help. No hope."

"Until you came along. Are you sure she wasn't setting you up?"

"You know me better than that."

"I used to think I knew you."

Silence fell until she whispered, "I can't ignore what I found. Please help. I need someone I can trust."

"Trust." He let the word hang.

"Someone who doesn't freeze when things get ugly," Sable insisted, ignoring the atmosphere between them. "Someone who knows how I work."

"Someone who shared your bed?"

"Don't twist this—"

"Any more than you have already?"

Her lips thinned. "Take us out of it. This is business, Elijah."

"Glad we got that straight. So, what's the intel?" His sweeping glance told her the church was empty for now, but wouldn't stay so for long.

"I've got everything we need to burn their operation. Names. Faces. Routes. Contacts. But…"

"They're watching you," he concluded as she hesitated. "Which means they're watching me. We can't talk here."

"Where?"

"My yacht. The *Seraphim* is moored in Grand Harbour."

"Your space. Your rules."

"I'm still alive," he pointed out.

"When?"

"Follow me out. Say a prayer first. From the sound of it, we'll need all the help we can get."

He slipped through a side door, back into the sun and the reassuring bustle of a busy street. She would follow. The mission mattered too much for Sable to run now.

Did he want her to follow him? Did he want to wake the past?

Fuck it!

Why not? The cause was bigger than both of them.

CHAPTER THREE

She did as he asked, and even said a prayer, though it seemed impertinent to ask a supreme being she wasn't even sure she believed in to help her succeed in the mission, but it couldn't hurt to ask for help on others' behalf. God knew they needed it. "Help the captives survive until we get there, and restrain the cruel hand of the slavers."

Now she only had Elijah to face.

Great.

Leaving the hard wooden pew behind, she walked swiftly and silently to her prechosen exit. The main thing to remember, she reassured herself as she stepped out into the heat of the busy street, was not to flinch or beg for his help. Not a single flicker of doubt must cross her face. If Elijah knew how terrified she was at the thought of confronting this particular band of slavers, he might question why she'd come back, putting him and his team in danger.

It was a risk she was prepared to take to save Anna Marie and others like her.

That was only half the picture. Missing Elijah had been hell. Seeing him again for any length of time would be worse.

On a personal level, their relationship had been purely physical. Apart from his promise of a ring. That had been his one and only gesture of something more than sex. And how short-lived had that been. Chasing his brutal ghost had only made her more frustrated.

It wasn't all about sex. We laughed together too.

There was no sign of those rare, precious moments being repeated, nor would there ever be. She'd forfeited his trust when she left.

Missions had always ended in a vigorous celebration of life. Like that time in Sarajevo, she reflected as she approached the harbor. Rain had been coming down in sheets, yet they were on a rooftop with Elijah's fist in her hair. The delicious rhythm he set as thunder cracked overhead held her on the edge for ages. "You come when I say, not before," he'd instructed.

His thumb had circled her clit with cruel precision until she sobbed his name into the storm, begging for release. When he finally gave her what she wanted, she realized he'd remained ice-cold throughout.

That wouldn't happen again.

Really?

Given the chance, would I refuse?

Absolutely.

Better not put that to the rest.

She arrived at a stunning vantage point with the harbor laid out before her. The *Seraphim*, with its sinister black helicopters squatting on the top deck, was more than impressive. It was magnificent and intriguing. All the other flashier, smaller boats looked insignificant by comparison.

A shiver ran down her spine at the sight of Elijah's floating fortress moored like a ruling monarch in the biggest berth at the furthest end of the marina, with a security cordon around it.

Somewhere in that circle was Elijah.

Some nagging demon chose that moment to whisper into her head. Dark nights and darker passions. He'd always been inventive. Her wrists bound with his belt, his mouth between her thighs, and then that slow, deliberate claiming as she begged in two languages while he watched her break with ice-cold satisfaction.

This was the man she was about to confront.

When they'd shared a small apartment in Cospicua, one of the three ancient cities across the harbor from Valetta, Elijah came back from recon one night, wired and hungry. No words. He backed her against the wall, ripped off her clothes, and drove into her in one savage thrust.

The utter bliss of submitting to pleasure was a memory that had kept her awake on many a night since. Elijah always fucked her as if trying to brand himself into her bones.

But that had changed. She had changed. Now these memories served only as warnings. Elijah took what he wanted, then walked away.

I did that last time.

Her silent confession opened the floodgates, and another memory flashed into her mind. "You'll remember this every time you try to forget me," he'd said just before tipping her over the edge. He'd made her wait so long that the sensation was almost unbearable. She could remember it as if it were only moments ago, her body seizing around him as he held her pinned to the wall.

When she was calm again, he stayed inside her, his forehead pressed to hers. That was the closest he'd ever come to a tender gesture. She'd hoped he'd say more. And should have known better. Pulling out, he walked away as if nothing remarkable had happened.

How many more warnings did she need? If Elijah knew how many times she'd found release with his name on her lips— He'd do what? Laugh?

He wouldn't care.

Elijah was her drug and her damnation, and she was about to meet him again of her own free will.

Traffic chaos descended from the ramparts down to the harbor below. The discordant noise was a fitting soundscape for Black Meridian's vow of vengeance. The consortium's kill price for Elijah's head was in the multimillions, reflecting the danger he posed to their trillion-dollar operation.

Remaining with him would have made her a homing beacon, guiding Black Meridian to their target. Her disappearance, together with Elijah's strategic thinking, made the *Seraphim* appear to be nothing more than another megayacht owned by a shell corporation. His connection to the vessel had never been listed.

His survival was more important than her happiness, which was why she left. Only this brush with an innocent girl with no one else to defend her could persuade Sable to come out of hiding and put Elijah at risk. Anna Marie's story was so similar to theirs that she couldn't ignore it.

She stared at the *Seraphim*. The vessel was huge, like an armored city. Sable could never have imagined Elijah would own something like it when they first met as rookie agents.

Military technology was the source of his wealth. She guessed the hull was reinforced and the interior armored. Cutting-edge tech would be everywhere. The *Seraphim* was not some pampered billionaire's plaything, but a manifestation of power, control, and fearsome strength.

Fortress Elijah. Safer for his team and the people he'd

sworn to protect. Shock and awe directed at any enemy in his path.

Being this close to Elijah and his floating kingdom spooked the hell out of her. The outcome today was by no means certain, and from what she'd seen in the cathedral, Elijah was not in a forgiving mood. He'd treated her as if she were something he'd scraped off his boot.

She couldn't blame him. He'd believed she was dead, yet here she was, not just alive, but demanding more.

Would it change anything if he knew the truth, or would he be even angrier because she hadn't told him—

"Halt! This is a private dock."

A massive guard blocked her way. Dressed in black, he had to be one of Elijah's men. His build alone confirmed her suspicion that the *Seraphim* was more barracks than pleasure craft.

Keeping her voice low and level, she explained that Elijah Steel was expecting her.

"Name, ma'am?"

"Sable Alexandrovna."

He checked his tablet, then waved her on with an unexpectedly warm "Welcome aboard, Ms. Alexandrovna"

Something flickered in his eyes as she turned to acknowledge him. Surprise? Respect? Was she overthinking? Perhaps he'd heard rumors about her relationship with Elijah.

He paused for a beat, then stepped aside to allow her to approach the gangplank.

She stared up at the few short steps she would have to take to enter Elijah's world. It might as well have been a creaking footbridge over a crevasse. Firming her jaw, she took the first step.

A crew member in crisp whites waited at the top. "Ms.

Alexandrovna. Commander Steel is expecting you. Permit me to escort you."

Commander Steel? How appropriate. She almost smiled.

"Ms. Alexandrovna"

"Yes, of course. Sorry. I'm trying to take everything in."

Her escort's expression remained neutral. "Are you ready to move on?"

God help her, yes.

"Yes. Thank you."

Elijah was a dangerous obsession, but some obsessions weren't chains; they were oxygen, and she'd just taken her first free breath in a long time.

CHAPTER FOUR

His jaw tightened as Sable set foot on the deck. He was in his office onboard, one hip braced against the desk. Damn her for looking so small and vulnerable when he knew the opposite was true.

Against the vastness of his yacht, anyone would look small, he reassured himself.

But not so familiar.

Was that any surprise? They used to move like twin cogs in the same machine, seamless, balanced, unstoppable.

Seven years of believing her dead had ground that connection to dust. All he felt now was resentment. If she failed to convince him this mission was worth his attention, she could sort out her own fucking mess—

"Sir?"

"A moment, please."

The steward retreated. The quiet click of the door left him to contemplate a past he'd spent years burying. Sable moved as if she owned the ship. Head high, shoulders loose, her gaze scanning the corners the way they used to scan rooftops together. Every line of her body was a memory he'd tried to burn out of his blood.

Shifting position to ease the sudden pressure on the placket of his jeans, he let out a short, harsh laugh. Remembering how good they'd been in bed, or on a mission, was a pointless exercise. Seven years of iron control had taught him not to feel a damn thing.

Oh, yeah? Thirty seconds of Sable Alexandrovna on his deck had him hard enough to hammer steel.

Part of him admired her grit in coming to confront him—

Fuck, no.

Fuck, yes. She was a formidable adversary, lover, ghost. One glimpse of her in tight jeans and that goddamn baseball cap turned him into a weapon with the safety off.

He resented the hell out of the way she made him feel, his skin prickling as if she were already touching him. Resented how his hands remembered the exact weight of her hips and how his mouth knew the taste of her throat when she came undone. Resented that his body didn't give a damn that she'd put him through a living funeral—

A discreet knock on the door jolted him back to the present.

"Sir?"

He drew a breath and forced his shoulders to relax. "Send her in."

His erection throbbed in brutal agreement.

No one knew better than he that emotion was a liability. Being dumped in a shop doorway as a child might have something to do with that. Foster homes only cemented his belief that nothing lasted and no one could be trusted. Sable had proved it when she disappeared without a word.

He'd trusted only two women. The first was Mara, a young girl a couple of years older than him who had shielded him in one of the worst hellholes he'd ever encountered. Starvation and beatings had been the least of it. Fending off the sickening attention from both "mother" and "father" in that foster home had kept him pretty busy too.

Sable also had a rough history, most of which she kept back, he suspected, but that early pain was the glue that brought them together. Whatever her past, Sable had managed to find the bright side of life. She made him feel things he'd never experienced: fun, laughter, and light in the dark place they both inhabited.

That made her betrayal doubly inexcusable.

Enough reminiscing. It was time to interrogate the disruptor-in-chief.

The *Seraphim* was breathtaking. Her first impression was luxury taken to the nth degree, but the tingle down her spine suggested this was misleading. It was Elijah's vessel, after all.

Light poured in through floor-to-ceiling windows, revealing pale oak, brushed steel, and low, sculptural furniture in muted grays and creams. Gorgeous. And this was just the entrance. Low sofas dressed in linen and cashmere were in the best possible taste. A faint scent of cedar and the ocean pervaded the air. Everything was high-end, classy, and understated.

On closer inspection, she spotted hidden seams and invisible hinges—

"Ms. Alexandrovna"

"My apologies." There was just enough time to assess a series of panels too perfectly aligned to be mere decoration. She'd have given anything to know what lay beneath. Best guess? They concealed the vessel's true nature.

Best guess? Reinforced compartments housing tactical equipment. The *Seraphim* might be a sanctuary on the surface: calming, elegant, and exquisitely refined, but beneath the pale wood and quiet beauty throbbed the hull-deep hum of a battleship.

"The Grand Salon."

Her escort had paused to make the announcement. No wonder he felt he had to comment. The space was incredible. Turning slowly, she took in the soft cream kidskin seating, black marble surfaces, and the abundance of crystal goblets, safely stored in secure glass cabinets above the bar. The Grand Salon was designed to impress. It was easy to picture heads of state, oligarchs, and other mysterious clients with deep pockets and deeper problems standing exactly where she stood now. She'd still bet her life that the *Seraphim*'s deadliest fangs remained hidden.

The escort cleared his throat.

Taking the hint, she followed him to a lower deck, where luxury gave way to silence. The layout was sparser and more practical. The only sound was the faint hum of the engines. No crew was visible, yet the prickling awareness of surveillance suggested she was being watched.

Cameras everywhere, she reminded herself. And, somewhere close by, a control room where her every move would be monitored.

Elijah's army was probably cleaning rifles, studying maps and satellite images, or running drills behind armored doors. Brushing her hand across the wall's smooth, cool surface, she could only guess at the number of sensors and bulletproof tech beneath.

Elijah left nothing to chance.

The *Seraphim* was an iceberg, glittering and showy above the waterline, but with a lethal killer instinct beneath.

Determination surged through her as she pictured the captives in their cells. How different life was for them. Chains chafing their skin as they endured stench and terror, with no guarantee of a better future. She would remain on Elijah's yacht until she had his firm commitment to undertake the mission. He'd have to set aside whatever he thought of her. Too many innocent lives were at stake.

They entered another, more populated part of the ship where tough-looking individuals in black tactical gear ignored them.

The closer she came to Elijah, the more apparent the *Seraphim*'s true purpose became. His floating fortress was a perfect representation of one man's indomitable will. Complex and highly intelligent, who else could rise from squalor to create such a formidable force? And then, to help as many people as possible, present the *Seraphim*, his most powerful weapon, as a spoiled billionaire's playground.

Elijah was a master of deception, she remembered, pulse rising as she thought back to a mission when anyone but he might have sought shelter, safe in the knowledge that the danger had passed.

Not Elijah.

His first instinct was to set aside the fact that only minutes before, they'd been under fire, to twist his fist in her hair. Yanking her close, he turned her to face away from him. Removing whatever clothes were necessary to achieve his aim, he thrust deep with slow, deliberate strokes.

The filth that had poured from her mouth on that occasion…

Better not think of it now.

Thunderclaps had masked her cries of pleasure as his forefinger circled her clit with cruel precision. Tightening his grip, he had insisted, "Not until I tell you." Then he held her on the brink for what felt like forever. When he finally growled, “Come now,” she had needed no encouragement. Clenching around him, bucking like a bronco, she had both given and taken some of the best sex ever. But once again, when it was over, she realized that he’d remained ice-cold throughout.

“Ms. Alexandrovna”

“Yep—” Hurrying through the door her companion had opened, she tried to stay focused, but with Elijah on her mind that was a struggle.

One she eventually lost.

Pristina: Kosovo’s largest city. Naked on the bed in their small apartment, with her wrists lashed to the headboard. A single black candle cast a flickering shadow across Elijah’s face as he spread her wide. His tongue was relentless as he held her open while she writhed and pleaded for release. When he finally rose over her, his eyes were stern, demanding complete cooperation. Braced, he entered her slowly and deliberately, making sure she felt every inch of him along the way. “Watch me,” he’d ordered, voice arctic.

He took her over the edge with deep, satisfying strokes. “Hold your legs wide,” he instructed at one point. “Concentrate—that place is your world.”

He knew how much she loved watching. How often had it been like that—no prep, no mercy, no emotion?

Could raw, animal possession ever be enough?

No.

Why had she tolerated such a cold, unfeeling man?

Because their roots were the same?

Yes.

They had been planted in the same barren patch. And she liked sex. She liked sex with Elijah. Her problem was that she loved him and doubted he could ever feel the same. He was the missing piece in a jigsaw unlikely ever to be completed.

That last night in Malta, while she was still recovering from amazing sex, he pulled out and set her down like discarded gear, then turned away to strip his weapons.

"Nearly there—"

"What? Oh, sorry…" The wake-up call from her escort was another reminder that memories of Elijah were dangerously distracting and that being here had nothing to do with reconciling with a man as cold as he was deadly.

It was purely business.

Anna's wide-eyed terror flashed into her mind, along with silent processions of lost souls on their journey to hell. No one else had the manpower and know-how to free them. Guilt twisted inside her at the thought of being distracted on a personal level when she needed Elijah for very different reasons now.

"Sable—"

She should have been prepared for this. Hearing his voice sucked the air from her lungs. Spinning around, she lifted her chin to face him. A sinister sight, as dark and rough as his voice, danger wrapped Elijah in lethal stillness.

"Welcome to the *Seraphim*."

"Elijah." She sounded so matter-of-fact. *Well done, me!* He was everything she remembered from the cathedral and more: broad-shouldered, cold-eyed, with no softness in his posture or manner.

Recovering quickly, she gestured around, "This is impressive. It's good of you to agree to this meeting."

"It's a fucking miracle," he snarled.

"Since I'm dead?"

Ignoring her, he led the way down a stark, unadorned corridor. The business end of the vessel was exactly as she had suspected: functional and fortified. He opened a door to a large, high-tech office where monitors glowed and the air hummed with intent. “May I?” she asked, tipping her chin toward the screens.

“Go ahead.”

She moved past him. Too close. His scent curled around her, warm and clean, hitting her senses like a punch.

“Since you’re here, you might as well make yourself comfortable.”

Every tiny hair on the back of her neck stood on end as he came to stand behind the chair she chose. Arms folded, remote, he was a living testament to everything she’d lost.

“Okay?” he demanded brusquely when she shivered involuntarily.

“I’m fine.” She made the mistake of meeting his gaze. He read her instantly. His stony expression was the best reminder yet not to drift into sentiment. Whatever they’d shared was ash. Straightening her spine, she plunged in. “If the situation I’ve uncovered weren’t dire, I wouldn’t bother you with it.”

“You’d have stayed dead?”

The scorn in his words cut deep.

Worse, they were true.

CHAPTER FIVE

Muted lighting cast a low amber haze over his study. Monitors added to the glow, their light framing Sable in a misleading halo. She'd never been an angel. After seven years of silence, who would trust her now?

Then she did that thing.

The curve of her mouth. The barest flick of her tongue across her lower lip. It shouldn't affect him, yet it did. He'd have to be carved from stone not to react to a woman he'd taken to battle and bed.

He had to remind himself that she was a stranger to him now. As such, she would be judged on merit, not memory.

Time had been kind to Sable, at least in looks. Her inner radiance remained. Was the quicksilver mind intact? His best guess was yes. Her fierce spirit shone in her eyes. "Don't make me regret this meeting."

"You won't," she promised, gaze steady.

"Coffee?"

"Please."

He filled two mugs. Sable was careful not to brush his

hand as she took hers. Good. Being close enough to catch her scent was dangerous.

Her manner was unmarked by the years that had gouged wounds in him. Trust was something he rarely gave, and he'd made an exception for Sable. One he had lived to regret. "Are you using me?" he asked as they sipped.

"In some ways, yes," she admitted, nursing her mug. "I didn't know what else to do—whom else to turn to."

"You're asking me to risk my team on the word of someone I no longer trust."

"You can trust me," she protested.

"Can I? Where did you go? Why did you leave? Why couldn't you speak to me first?" He cut her off as she began to answer. "Spare me excuses. Just tell me what you need."

She took a flash drive from her pocket. "This explains most things."

Once again, she was careful not to touch him as she handed it over. "Well?" she pressed. "Don't you want to review it?"

"I'll take a look."

The images on screen confirmed the atrocities Sable had hinted at. He could no longer remain impartial. Humanity, or the mockery of it, always found new ways to degrade itself.

"Sick, yes?" she said, briefly turning to face him.

He couldn't speak for a moment as the foulest form of child exploitation was revealed. There were other images: women working beyond endurance until their hands bled, young men who must dearly wish to be old and ugly rather than young and beautiful. As often as he saw proof of man's inhumanity to man, he never lost the will to act. The only time he hit a wall was with his own feelings.

"You okay?" Sable asked, shooting him a concerned glance. "This is a lot."

"I need air." Gripping the back of his neck, he walked out on deck. Slavers were an infestation that was impossible to wipe out, but that was no reason not to try.

Sable followed and came to stand silently at his side. The repeated slap of water against the hull only fueled his impatience to free the people he'd seen on the screen. Every second wasted was a second lost to the victims.

"Do you think we'll be in time?"

She must have read his thoughts. "Coordinates?" She gave them, and he called the bridge.

"Elijah?" Her voice was softer than he'd ever heard it, yet her jaw was set iron strong.

The steel in her soul had always impressed him. "This mission has just become vital to both of us."

"Black Meridian is expanding fast. Malta, Libya, Odessa, Eastern Europe—they're everywhere. It's a very efficient supply chain."

"I don't care what they are, what they have. We'll deal with them."

"We?" she repeated.

"The team," he made clear before she could get any ideas.

There was a pause, and then she said, "There's more."

Their stares locked. "Oh?"

"They know about you—the *Seraphim*, your jet, the helicopters, and the forces you command. They've marked you for elimination."

He gave a dry snort. "I'd be insulted if they ignored me."

"That means you're in?"

"Didn't I just say that? Tell me why you chose me when there are other mercenary groups you could have picked."

"You're the best, and I trust you. And you know one of the captives on the auction list."

"Who?" he demanded.

"A woman called Mara."

Ice gripped his spine. "You know this how?"

"I hacked an encrypted auction site. No names. Just images of the upcoming lots. I recognized Mara from that picture you carry, the one with two kids on a riverbank. Taken maybe fifteen years ago? Mara was a pretty child, but now she's a beautiful woman."

He remembered the day the shot was taken by neighbors who took pity on the foster children next door. He'd been holding up a fish he and Mara had caught with a hair clip and a piece of twine. They'd wanted to pay the neighbors back for their kindness. Desperation and hunger forced them to try anything, and on that day, they'd caught a fish.

Their so-called parents at the time ran their "happy" home like a business, taking in as many children as they could to make a profit. And now Mara was in danger, close enough to rescue. "You sure about this?"

"I'm positive," Sable said firmly.

Anger boiled inside him. "Where is this auction?"

"A small island off Malta. Remote. Cameras everywhere. Security will be tight."

"I like a challenge."

"Don't you mean you thrive on the impossible?"

"I partnered up with you."

"True," she conceded wryly.

"What's this island called?"

"It doesn't have a name. It's barely big enough to be more than a rock."

He called the bridge. "Hold our position offshore when we arrive. Engage dynamic positioning." He turned to Sable. "That will keep the *Seraphim* fixed at one GPS location without anchoring."

"Fast getaway?" she suggested.

"Correct. If you want to leave, you'd better go now."

"Jump overboard?" she suggested.

His crew was a well-oiled machine. The *Seraphim* was already underway.

"Like a ghost slipping away in the night," Sable murmured, staring over the side as they headed for the open sea.

"Like you?" he suggested.

"Harder to vanish at sea—unless you throw me overboard."

"Don't tempt me."

The tension had eased a little between them. Whatever Sable's past actions, ensuring the success of a mission would always come first. And she was good. Better than good, she could be a game changer in a situation where she knew more than most.

Learning that Mara was involved added urgency to the plan developing in his mind. "I'll have a steward show you to your quarters."

"Thank you."

He'd already turned away, job done. It was only when she left that he realized Sable's energy had gone with her. The room felt bigger, emptier, and colder.

It was hard to say what pissed him off more—wanting her or shutting her out.

CHAPTER SIX

She didn't go straight to her room. Instead, she diverted her escort with a blatant lie. "The commander asked me to visit the armory to choose whatever I need for the mission."

"Certainly, ma'am. This way, please."

He escorted her down two flights of narrow steps ending in a long corridor lined with steel doors. This was Elijah's reality. The rest of the *Seraphim* was a facade: sleek, luxurious, and carefully curated to both mislead and reassure guests.

Her companion used iris recognition to unlock the door. "Do I need someone to sign out the weapons?"

"What do you think?"

Elijah's cold voice pierced her spine. Of course, he knew what she'd done. Cameras were everywhere.

The officer had already gone, leaving Elijah in his place, and he looked more threatening than ever. All muscle and ice, he stared down from his great height as if she were the enemy.

"You can hardly stop now," he said, as she began to make

excuses in order to leave and choose a better time to inspect the armory.

How could I possibly have made love with this man?

Love? They'd collided like feral creatures wolfing down a reward.

"I'm sorry. I should have asked you first before coming down here."

"As you're here now…"

His eyes were like ice chips, but she met his gaze calmly. "I'm not sorry for letting curiosity get the better of me," she admitted as the steel door hissed shut behind them, sealing them in a climate-controlled space.

"I trust you'll find everything you need?"

Wow. Would she ever.

She gazed around at an impressive display of weaponry. Stacked on steel shelves, the inventory was as neatly ordered as Elijah's mind had grown. "You used to be reckless," she murmured as she examined the arsenal. "One handgun and a knife."

"Three knives," he corrected her. "One you could see—"

"And two concealed about your person."

"Correct. But that was then, and this is now."

"And now control is your thing." Her lips tightened into a line of approval as she walked down his arcade of death.

"Control keeps me alive."

The sealed room was ordered and lethal. This was the domain of a man who was no longer a young fighter but a hardened strategist, honed by experience, and backed by sufficient wealth to support a private army.

"You approve?"

"Do you care?"

He shrugged. "Not really."

Lounging against the wall, arms folded, he watched her inspection with a predatory stillness that set her senses on fire. Pheromones rolled off him, clashing with hers to create a vortex of tension that showed no sign of easing up.

She gasped involuntarily as he pushed off the wall. Elijah's magnetism was overpowering. However cold he appeared, the charge between them was white-hot.

I hate that I want him—want it, want sex.

Subtle lighting carved harsh shadows beneath his cheekbones and across his jaw, where sharp black stubble, the same stubble she remembered abrading her skin, made him look like a marauding pirate.

Maraud away, she thought, wondering whether any woman with red blood in her veins could remain composed under these circumstances. Elijah could always tell when she was ready to mate, which used to be all the time he was around.

He halted when they were toe-to-toe. Her breathing faltered, and her body went on full alert. But he reached past to select a sidearm from its stand on the wall. "You're gonna love this. It's better than anything you've used before."

It took her a moment to speak. Why did she fall for this every time? The faint flare of amusement in his eyes told her he knew how he affected her. "Thanks for the suggestion," she said, proud of her steady voice. "I take it you've got a firing range where I can test this?"

"Of course."

Was he playing her?

Bastard.

He knew what made her tick—what used to make her tick for him.

"This is all very impressive." She scanned the deadly gallery behind him: matte-black rifles, polished pistols, and steel blades resting in foam mounts. "You've come a long way."

"As have crime and criminals."

"And this?" She glanced at the locked compartment with its skull-and-bones insignia.

"Drones and other high-tech killing machines."

Her stomach clenched. She was dragging him back into danger. Had she just wasted seven years?

The brutal answer was yes.

"I've seen enough. Thank you." She needed to escape this museum of death and breathe fresh air.

Too eager to leave, she bumped into him.

They collided hard, like running into a brick wall.

He dipped his head.

She looked up.

Their mouths clashed in a kiss that knocked the stuffing out of all her carefully made pledges. Whatever had happened in the past was irrelevant. His fist tangled in her hair, drawing her head back. Devouring her mouth, he kissed her throat, then the lobes of her ears, before driving his mouth down on hers.

Hardly a passive recipient, she slammed him into the steel cabinets, making the weapons rattle a tattoo. His hands found her hips, gripping and positioning. Yanking her hard against the thrust of his erection catapulted her back into the past. Heat roared between them—

But it wasn't the past.

And everything was broken.

Elijah tore away first.

"I trusted you," he raged, swiping the back of his hand across his mouth as if to erase all trace of her. "Do you have any idea what that means? No," he bit out before she could reply. "You knew I couldn't refuse this mission, but don't make the mistake of thinking you can walk back into my life."

It hadn't started out that way. She'd have done anything to avoid involving him in an operation deadlier than most, but she couldn't let the slavers win or save their victims on her own.

Things were rapidly going downhill with Elijah. His expression said she was teetering on the brink. Desperate to salvage the situation, she said, "Trust doesn't come easily for either of us, but it grew when we worked together. I know it can happen again."

"You destroyed trust!"

"I'm determined to rebuild it." She had no idea how, yet, with the taste of him still on her lips, and the imprint of his body on hers burning into her soul.

"How do you propose to do that?" he challenged. "By attempting to seduce me?"

"*What?* I'm not interested."

"Not yet," he derided.

Why had she ever thrown herself at a man who clearly didn't want her, who offered nothing but sex? She had wanted more—she still did: more emotion, more connection, a life that didn't involve violence and danger and sex.

Seven years ago, that knowledge had almost destroyed her. Tomorrow, she would fight with everything she had to save those without the power to defend themselves. To succeed in that mission, it was vital to forget wanting Elijah.

"Time to call a halt," she said briskly. "I'd like to try out this weapon at your shooting range—if you'll show me the way."

"I think you mean *you* should call a halt to this," Elijah countered scathingly. "I'll have someone show you where you need to go."

"Thank you." Her tone was clipped, but her pulse was off the scale. He was ice. She was fire. She had to get away—

She blundered into the corridor the instant the steel door opened. The lighting was merciless, like a spotlight on a stage. Her swollen lips and red cheeks were obvious to anyone.

"May I assist you?"

Could her face get any hotter? The ever-polite escort had just appeared on the scene. "My stateroom, please." The shooting range could wait. She had to calm down first.

"Of course, ma'am. Please follow me."

Not a flicker in his eyes betrayed that he knew exactly what had happened in the armory. There were cameras everywhere. The whole ship almost certainly knew.

With the most challenging mission of her career about to begin, she was still obsessing over the fact that Elijah could unmake her with a kiss.

That had to change.

Fast.

Worse—she'd let him kiss her.

Worse still, she'd do it again.

~

What the fuck…

He didn't breathe until the door shut behind her. Her scent lingered, keeping him hard. Tearing away from Sable was not rejection. It was survival.

Bracing his hands against the wall, he exhaled hard. Try as he might to reject the memories, they pressed in: Sable laughing on warm nights, her dress slipping off one shoulder. The defiant tilt of her chin, the way she leaned into him with equal parts surrender and challenge. Her mouth, soft, demanding, unforgettable.

Was recovery even possible?

No matter how many times he told himself it was just physical, they weren't saints and had healthy appetites—he'd never found another woman like her.

No one came close.

CHAPTER SEVEN

The opulence of her stateroom failed to capture Sable's attention, though she listened politely as the steward enumerated its many features, ending with "I trust everything is to your liking."

His tone suggested that walking the plank was the option if she found fault. "It's perfect. Thank you." She didn't have a clue, and it was a relief when the door closed behind the steward.

She scanned the room for cameras. Old habits die hard. It also gave her a chance to get her head straight after the encounter with Elijah.

Easier said than done.

What the hell was wrong with her? She was here to enlist Elijah's help, not shag him senseless.

With the camera scan and listening device check complete, she flopped onto the bed. Now she allowed herself to appreciate the stylish decor. Soft neutrals, clean lines, everything she liked. The bed, dressed in crisp white linen, was huge and inviting. A console across the room held an array of freshly squeezed juices, together with still and sparkling water.

Plus bar nibbles.

She could use a bite. Leaving the bed to explore what was on offer, she chose a fat, juicy olive and wandered out onto the private deck. Nice. There wasn't much to see at night, other than the bow of the moon and a scattering of stars, but it was quite an experience to be safely housed on a luxury vessel cutting through rolling black water at speed.

Leaning over the rail, she scanned the ocean, fathomless and impenetrable like Elijah. She touched her lips. Still swollen. Still his.

Get your head straight, dumb klutz! She'd be working with the entire Blood and Thunder team, not just Elijah. She'd be meeting them for the first time, and first impressions mattered. Distraction wasn't an option.

But she'd be in the same space as the man who'd kissed her senseless—

Tough shit. Suck it up.

The atmosphere shifted the moment Sable walked in. She might be tiny compared with the formidable-looking men at the top of the Blood and Thunder team, but she had a presence that commanded everyone's attention. For the right reasons. There was nothing frivolous about Sable.

She picked a seat between Cesar and Alexei, possibly the two most unfriendly-looking men, and didn't seem to notice their suspicious stares. Cesar, possibly Cuban, who the hell knew, was definitely dangerous and unknowable to everyone but his life partner, Mica, a Krav Maga specialist who would be joining the team for this mission. Alexei, a Russian oligarch known for ruthlessly dispatching anyone foolish enough to go up against him, was married. Would he trust him around Sable? Not a chance. He wouldn't trust either man where Sable was concerned.

Why should he care?

Apparently, he did.

Male ego and testosterone speaking, he concluded, giving the nod for Sable to begin.

She smoothly took over the briefing. Maps and satellite images flickered across the screen. Terrified children with huge eyes, alongside cowering men and women, devoid of hope. All were dressed in rags, though that would change at the auction.

The team remained grim faced throughout, though he knew from the restlessness around the table that they couldn't wait to begin the rescue mission.

"We're dealing with madmen," Sable told them.

"As always," Cesar observed.

Cesar was a little mad himself, but in a good way, not like this foul proof of evil.

"They'll be hosed down in freezing water before the auction, then dressed up like K-Pop stars," Dante, the guy they called the Romani chieftain, growled as silence fell over the meeting, heavy and dark.

"That's the end of the presentation," Sable announced, lifting the atmosphere with her positive attitude. "Questions?"

She fielded several technical queries. "Time to move," she said then. "Let's send these fuckers straight to hell."

CHAPTER EIGHT

They used rubber raiding boats, Elijah's preferred choice for silent insertions. The team slipped overboard the instant the engines cut. Weapons raised, they waded through the shallows, making swift progress toward a stony beach.

The sky was black overhead. No moon or stars lit their way. Silent offshore, the *Seraphim* was invisible behind an outcrop of rock.

Night goggles let them spot the drainage tunnel they were heading for. Mica stayed with the boats to provide supporting fire if the mission went to hell.

Elijah led, his hands slicing through the dark to direct the team. Sable covered him, their old rhythm reinstated as if it had never paused.

The team froze in place when he raised a fist.

Elijah beckoned Sable forward, the two of them taking point as they moved down the dank, oppressive tunnel. It wasn't long before they found the first cage. Conditioned to expect danger, the occupants shrank into each other. He reassured them with the universal sign for peace. Hands clawed through the bars, so he returned the first V-sign reversed with a fist to his heart in a pledge of support and rescue.

Retracing his steps while Sable, speaking several languages, reassured the captives, he waved the team on. The tunnel ended at the foot of a flight of stone steps. At the top was a torch-lit courtyard. Beyond it, a grand, if dilapidated, building glowed obscenely bright.

A stage dominated a room of well-dressed buyers sipping champagne. Barefoot girls dressed as biblical slaves in scratchy hessian robes served drinks to the leering punters. Chandeliers that had seen better days sparkled above them, casting a crazed light over threadbare red velvet seats, while their occupants laughed and gossiped as if the slaves they were waiting to see were merely another luxury item, like jewelry or designer clothes.

It was a sickening sight and a call to action, but he signaled to the team to stay in place for now.

Sable waited tensely for Elijah's signal. The sale had begun, each precious life reduced to a number in a catalog. Stumbling onstage, shielding their eyes from the spotlight, the victims were mocked by the crowd, as a glitter-drenched viper served as auctioneer.

The only good thing about the escalating noise was that it served as a helpful distraction. At Elijah's signal, Sable and the team mounted the roof and then climbed down to the upper gallery overlooking the scene.

Finding a place, she slipped into the shadows. Each crack of the gavel was like a blow that fueled her fury. Her jaw ached from clenching in impatience to begin.

"And now the star of tonight's collection…"

The room fell silent as two burly guards dragged a young woman into the light.

Mara.

Dressed in silk and jewels, with golden shackles on her wrists and ankles, she had dark circles beneath beautiful eyes that burned with defiance. Proud, furious, and unbroken, her courage was plain to see.

"You can see her spirit," the auctioneer crowed. "Imagine taming this one." She paused for a sickening laugh. "Shall we say a hundred thousand to start?"

The first bid was a million. As the room erupted, Elijah took it as the signal to make his move. Weapon raised, body tense, only Sable's hand on his arm stopped him. "No emotion," she warned. "Wait for the gavel," she added as the bidding for Mara continued.

A counterbid of one million five drew gasps from the audience, but with no further bids, the auctioneer paused to confirm. Big mistake. The clap of the gavel coincided with Elijah abseiling from the balcony, firing from the waist as he dropped.

The scene descended into chaos. Surprise had always been the team's deadliest weapon. Mara had the good sense to dive for cover as black-clad Blood and Thunder operatives hit the ground like a plague of shadows.

Team members hustled captives toward the tunnel while Elijah blew out the chandeliers, raining glass on the remaining buyers. Sable moved through the scrum with predatory grace, cutting down hostiles with boot, blade, or bullet, while her colleagues cleaned up the rest.

Crossing the ballroom in a blur with Dante close behind, Elijah grabbed Mara by the arm. Hustling her toward safety, he was stopped by Sable's warning cry. A hostile had him in their crosshairs. Sable dropped the enemy with a clean shot.

For an instant, her gaze locked with Elijah's, but then another wave of slavers surged from the back of the hall.

Mara was cowering behind a pillar, hands over her head. Scooping her up, Elijah ran, firing at the enemy while Sable provided covering fire—until a charging hostile took her out.

Dumping Mara into another team member's arms, Elijah returned to snatch Sable out of danger.

"Thank you."

"Always."

He didn't stick around to waste words. There were padlocks to blast off the cages and a cleanup to finish in the hall.

Survivors who hadn't been chosen for the auction poured out of their squalid confinement. Shaking and exhausted, they were at least alive.

Once again a team of two, Elijah and Sable took up the rear to ensure no straggler, victim, or slaver was left unaccounted for. A scream drew Sable's attention back to the old building, where Anna Marie was being dragged by her hair. "Cover me!" Elijah barked.

She took out the thug holding Anna with sniper precision, but as she reset, a brute built like a brick wall launched himself, slamming her against a pillar, his blade at her throat. She ducked, but the angle was wrong.

Elijah was back.

Cracking the three of them into a wall, he sent the thug's knife skittering across the floor. Kicking it away, he yanked Sable clear.

"You've been hit!" she exclaimed, gasping for breath after her winding.

"Let me deal with this first," he warned.

He chose his strike well. The thug wouldn't trouble them again.

"You saved us," Anna gasped as Sable supported the shaking girl.

"Saved both of us," Sable added.

"Leave it," Elijah snapped when Sable attempted to take a look at the wound beneath his blood-soaked tunic.

"You're leaking all over me," she retorted, resorting to humor.

"What's new, honey?"

"Idiot! Don't you dare die on me!"

Thankfully, medics had arrived to help Anna to the boats, and, with a quick hug, the two women parted. The first-aid crew ignored Elijah. Would they dare suggest he needed help?

He must have read her mind. Was that a smile on his face? Cheeky fucker! "You should have gone with them. Can you walk?"

"You gonna carry me?"

Ignoring that, she turned practical. "I need to get you back. That wound needs immediate attention."

"I can walk, run, and fuck. Which would you like me to do first?"

"Add 'off' to the last option," she suggested.

The explosion ripped the night apart. Heat punched their backs. Throwing themselves into the tunnel, they covered their heads as everything behind them turned to fire and thunder.

Dragging her close, Elijah became her shield as dust rained down. "You look like a ghost," he growled, pulling back to stare into her face.

"You don't look so good yourself," she pointed out.

"Thankfully, I'm very much alive," he retorted, wiping soot from his mouth.

His hand remained firm on her waist, reminding every sense she had of what it felt like to be wanted by Elijah. But this was just safety in the field, she reminded herself. Nothing more guaranteed.

And who was to blame for that?

"That wound needs a dressing now," she insisted, reaching for her pack.

"There'll be time for that later. These people need care first."

"Which you won't be able to give if you're dead," she said, following Elijah's gaze to where the captives stood.

"Sable! Move the fuck on!" As he spoke, another blast shook the tunnel, and flames poured from its mouth. Tucking her under his arm, he ran.

"Where would I be without you bleeding all over me?" she gasped when Elijah finally set her down safely distant.

But this was no time for banter. The rescued were huddled on the shoreline, bewildered, waiting to be escorted—maybe to another hell, for all they knew.

"Our priority is to reassure these people and get them to safety," Elijah told her. "Then we can talk. In fact, you can do anything you want when we get back."

With blood soaking through his clothes? "I'll bandage you up. Then you can reassure the prisoners without frightening them half to death."

"Fearsome sight, me? They've seen worse."

She huffed with amusement. "You think?"

CHAPTER NINE

The *Seraphim* throbbed beneath his feet like a living beast. Built to outrun, outmaneuver, and outfight, she was a sanctuary for the rescued and his true north, the one constant that never failed him. Stocked with medical supplies and with surgeons onboard to tend the wounded, she had every facility the returning team required and more.

Sable worked tirelessly alongside him as they triaged the rescued. She nagged him about his wound. He refused treatment. That could wait. There was too much to do. He'd rest when the last of the prisoners had been assessed and cared for.

Medics were everywhere, comforting the broken and reassuring children who clutched at strangers as they cried for their parents. The hardest thought to banish was that their kin were likely dead, but keeping things positive was vital for the children to survive and eventually thrive.

The air on deck stank of blood and unwashed bodies, overlaid with a powerful disinfectant. "Get these people inside as soon as you can, to rest and be fed," he told the doctor in charge. "They need comfort and reassurance most of all."

"If we've seen worse, I can't think when," Sable told him as they met briefly. "Don't think I've forgotten," she added, her gaze fixed on the blood soaking through his tunic.

Okay, so it was bleeding again. Grudgingly, he stopped treating others and became a patient, but only when he was sure most of their shattered guests had been taken to more comfortable surroundings.

"If you lose any more blood, you'll be no use to anyone," Sable scolded as he led the way.

"Yeah, yeah."

Once inside his quarters, she cleaned the wound thoroughly, despite his repeated demands to get back on deck. Eventually, he'd had enough. "I can't do this—"

"You can and you will," she insisted, pushing him down again. "I know you feel guilty for taking time out, but nothing about this is how we'd like it. Those people need you alive and strong. So hold still, damn you, and let me finish!"

The instant she put her kit down, he was off.

"Hey! Come back," she called after him. "You can't go straight back. You could faint."

"Faint," he repeated, bringing his face close.

"You need to rest," she said, finding something to do rather than stay close to him.

"Have you ever known rest?"

Her cheeks pinked, telling him everything he needed to know about ever-so-practical, apparently detached Sable Alexandrovna. How long was she going to keep up the act? "I'm going to see Mara. Thanks for this. Much appreciated. You can find your own way back."

"I could find my way to hell and back," she assured him.

"Let's hope that's not necessary."

He closed the door on who the fuck knew which version of Sable: calm and cold, or hot and hungry? Did he care?

Fuck yes, he cared. And cared more every minute.

She took time off from her duties for one vital mission. Elijah had waited a long time to properly reunite with Mara, and she didn't want to miss it. There was a chance Mara might not want to be reminded of the past. Elijah was tough, but she'd seen him look at that photograph, as if it drove him to go further and work harder to help those who couldn't help themselves.

At least he'd finally let Sable take care of his outward wound. As for his inner turmoil? She doubted anyone could predict how that would end. If she had any part to play in his future, she'd like to help him heal.

If he'd allow that, which she doubted.

At least he'd survived. So had all the team members, none seriously injured. Thank God for that. It could have been so much worse.

She took a last look around to make sure she'd cleaned up the medical bits and pieces, then gathered her belongings and left to see who she could help next.

The deck was nearly empty when he arrived to search for Mara. The crew was tidying up, and a quiet calm had settled over the ship. The engines were steady, and it was a good time to think, to confide. All the lights were low, and the vastness of the sea swallowed inconsequential noise.

And then he saw her.

Standing by the rail, Mara stared out to sea. She didn't lean or sit, because standing and staying alert was safer. Spine straight, chin raised, weight evenly balanced on the balls of her feet, she was ready for anything.

Like him.

She seemed smaller than at the auction, and her long black hair was a mess after the chaos of the rescue, yet her hands, those no-nonsense hands he remembered so well from when she'd crafted toys from trash for him, were relaxed and steady at her sides.

He made a quick calculation that Mara must be thirty now. Her face was sharper, all angles and endurance. Simple gray sweats and borrowed sneakers took him back to the past, when new clothes were unknown to the two forgotten children.

She knew he was there. Instinct told Mara what her eyes couldn't see.

He clenched his fists and didn't relax until she turned and walked toward him. Halting in front of him, she lifted her chin, searching his eyes. "Elijah." Her voice was soft and calm. "I knew you'd save me."

"Your strength saved you."

A faint smile acknowledged it, and they embraced.

Mara's relief was obvious, while his concern only deepened. She was too thin and had seen too much. God only knew what she'd endured.

"Long time," he breathed. He didn't ask how she'd been, because that was painfully obvious. "How did you get here?" he asked instead.

"When I aged out of the foster system, like you, I had no safety net, family, or money. I bounced between low-paid jobs, cleaning, waitressing, and warehouse shifts. Rent for my single room had spiked, so I answered an ad for hospitality work overseas—good pay, travel covered. It sounded so exciting…"

"I'm sure," he said gently when she trailed off.

"The job never existed," Mara continued in a flat voice. "My passport was taken 'for safekeeping' on my arrival in Malta."

"They took your passport?" His jaw tightened. "They preyed on the wrong woman."

"The 'agency' turned out to be a trafficking front. By the time I realized that, I was already off-grid—one of the many 'disappeared.' I was moved through encrypted networks and sold on, I arrived at the auction where you found me." She laughed without humor. "Auction lot named: Ass ten. Prime stock."

He cursed inwardly. "You survived. That's all that matters."

"Thanks to you."

"You don't owe anyone gratitude for that. Not me, that's for sure. You're free thanks to *your* courage and resilience."

"You're angry."

"Does it show?"

"Fists clenched? Jaw tight? Yes, it shows. I know you, remember?"

They shared a quick smile.

Life had been shit for Mara, but when they pulled apart, her steady appraisal told him she hadn't changed. She still put others before herself with an inner strength and determination he could only admire. Once she recovered, she'd be an ideal recruit for the Blood and Thunder team.

"The other prisoners told me no one would come," she said in the same quiet voice. "But I knew you wouldn't forget."

Something viselike loosened in his chest. If Sable hadn't

gotten in touch with him, he wouldn't even have known Mara was in danger. "Of course, I'm here, and I'm not going anywhere. How did you hear about the team?"

"Word spreads fast among the desperate." Smiling, she brightened. "I followed your rise every step of the way."

A rise he could never have made without this woman. He doubted he'd have survived childhood without her. Finding Mara again was a reminder that good people existed, and that maybe he shouldn't distance himself from everyone just because he could.

Her gaze fell to his chest. "You got careless?" she asked, cocking her head and giving him a look. "Were you reckless, Elijah?"

"What, me?"

She laughed. "Still the same Elijah."

"Always. And this is nothing," he insisted as she stared at his arm.

She checked the dressing anyway, force of habit, he supposed. "You have a great partner," she said. "Did she do this for you?"

"Sable is an integral part of the team again."

"And in your life again?"

Ignoring the question, he told her to rest.

"There's time enough to rest when I'm dead," she replied. "What I'm looking for is a new direction so I can help others as you helped me."

"You started that trend," he reminded her. "But, as it happens, I do have an opening in mind. We'll talk when things have settled."

"You're the one who should be resting," she insisted.

"I'm not a child now."

"I can see that," she agreed, laughing as she stepped back.

~

The reunion between Elijah and Mara was everything Sable had hoped for. It made her even more eager to find Anna Marie—

"Sable!"

"Anna?"

Her young friend ran toward her and then stopped short. Bitter experience had taught her caution. Her hands clenched and unclenched as she asked, "May I call you Sable?"

"You can call me anything you want." Exclaiming with relief, she dragged the teenager into her arms.

"You always spoke to me," Anna whispered against her neck. "You were the only one who ever noticed me."

Sable laughed softly. "You used to say, 'It's me' in that soft voice of yours whenever we met in that echoing stairwell—"

"The one that stank of oil and bleach," Anna remembered. Pulling away, she took a deep breath. "You saw me getting into the SUV. You suspected what was going on." Her eyes shone fierce and bright. "Why did it take you so long to find us?"

"I won't lie. I had ghosts to deal with and an elusive man to find."

It was as if Anna Marie had only been waiting for confirmation that Sable was human too. Throwing her arms around Sable, she said, "I can never thank you enough. I hoped you'd come, because you always looked at me as if I mattered."

"Of course, you matter. So much," Sable said fiercely. Closing her eyes, she knew that every bridge she'd burned was worth it to be here.

Stepping back, Anna Marie studied her face as if searching for cracks that bitter experience had taught her to look for. Finding none, she nodded once, sharp and decisive. "If I can ever do anything to help. I'm nearly nineteen, you know. I should be working, not idling away my time thinking back. I want to move forward. I want to work—do something positive with my life. Work with children, maybe."

"I do have a few ideas to run by you when everything settles down," Sable admitted.

"Please use me however you can. I'll never be able to repay you for what you've done—and not just for me."

They pressed their foreheads together briefly and let the moment hang. It was a precious time of silent promises with the *Seraphim* humming steadily beneath them.

CHAPTER TEN

Sable looked exhausted but happy. She stood by the rail with Anna Marie tucked under her arm. He was glad for the two women. The reunion had done them both good.

Wiping a hand down the front of his dirt-streaked vest, he thought they both looked a mess. Dust clung to Sable's boots, and there was blood on her sleeve—his, probably. But when she turned to look at him, her expression held hope, and that was all that mattered.

This mission, with its personal connection, had left them both raw. The harshness Sable wore like armor had cracked wide open, revealing a new light of relief and purpose. Her eyes were red with fatigue, but she never stayed broken for long. Exhaustion was the price of the job she did. Whenever possible, Sable carried the burden so others didn't have to.

The administrator in charge arrived to take Anna Marie aside for a discreet interview. It gave Elijah the chance to approach Sable and catch hold of her before she dropped.

"Get off me," she scolded halfheartedly. "I don't want your blood all over me."

"I'm more worried about you."

"Unnecessary," she stated fiercely.

"Even so…"

"Even so, nothing—"

Ignoring this, he steered her toward the door and didn't stop until they reached his stateroom. Once inside, he allowed her to re-dress his wound. She was the best of nurses, but a little brutal at times, with what he could only describe as a no-nonsense touch.

"Do you take pleasure in dripping iodine into the wound?" he demanded at one point.

"Ouch?" she suggested in a baby voice when he flinched.

"Yes. Fucking ouch."

She showed him no mercy until she finally stepped back to view her handiwork. "There," she said. "You can put your top back on now."

"My bloodied top?"

"Well, put something on," she insisted.

Elijah's naked torso wasn't the only reason she needed him to cover up. The ring hanging around his neck troubled her. Why was he wearing it? It couldn't be his mother's; he never knew her. Whose could it be that meant so much to him that he wore it on a chain around his neck?

Why do I care?

But she did.

He made her forget the ring with a sideways look that made her laugh. "Okay. You're beautiful. And you know it," she added snippily. "Even slashed halfway to hell, with enough bruises to persuade me you belong to some new race of purple people, you're easy on the eye."

"Are you too tired?"

"For what?" she demanded, knowing full well what he was getting at.

Recovery after a mission had always meant celebrating life, and that half smile of his made her want to—

Fuck?

Oh, yeah.

But she wasn't ready for that. Maybe she never would be again. "I'm sorry," she said, turning serious. "Really sorry for everything I put you through."

"That again?" Catching her wrist, Elijah pressed his thumb to her pulse. "So, you're alive. Who knew? You left. You died. You came back. What are you trying to do now? Pick a fucking lane, Sable."

"I wasn't aware I was doing anything."

"Apart from teasing your bottom lip with the tip of your tongue as if I'm the next thing on your menu."

"You flatter yourself."

"Do I?"

She pulled away. He leaned in, crowding her until her spine met the door. "Can you even explain why you left?"

Blood drained from her face. "Black Meridian put a death mark on your file."

"You think I didn't know?"

"They sent images of the two of us, promising that if we didn't stop hounding slavers, they'd take their time carving slices off you while I watched."

"Hmm. Nice."

"Is that all you have to say?"

He shrugged.

"Disappearing was all I could think of to keep you safe. Believe me, every day I remembered how we'd both been betrayed as children. The last thing I wanted was to do that to you again."

"You'd do anything to avoid hurting me?" he suggested.

"I'd do anything to prevent you from being killed."

There was silence until he said, "You think I wouldn't burn Black Meridian organization to ash for you? You should have told me what you planned."

"And have you stop me? They counted on me sticking around, making it easy to find you. I was determined not to give those goons that chance."

He knew Black Meridian. They were trouble on a massive scale and could have taken both of them out. Sable had prevented that. And he was blaming her?

Something inside him fractured. The slavers' evil and the grief for precious time lost fueled his hunger for Sable—not just for sex, but more, much more.

He touched the ring at his neck. "Do you know why I wear this?

She tensed. "No."

Cupping her jaw, he tilted her face to meet his gaze. "I bought it seven years ago, just before you left."

Silence. "For you."

Her breath faltered. "You never said—"

"You left."

"Before—"

"Before I could ask you to be my partner in every way there is—to be my wife."

"*Wife?*" she exclaimed.

"Is that such a stretch? I wanted forever. There was a time when I thought you did too."

"I'm supposed to guess from the chill you gave off?"

"Careful, not cold. I never promise anything I can't deliver. I had to be sure."

It would have been easier to understand this if the expression on Elijah's face had changed by even an iota. But he was still the hottest thing on two hard-muscled legs, and sometimes the universe decides.

Their mouths crashed together, punishment and absolution. Fabric ripped as they tore at each other's clothes. Once they were naked, he lifted her clear off the floor, and she locked her legs around his waist.

Maybe he needed proof she was still alive—alive to him. And maybe Sable needed reassurance that those seven years apart had been worth it. One hand fisted in her hair, he pressed her back against the wall, while the other palmed her breast. His thumbnail abraded her nipple. She gasped his name in a choking sob.

"Say it again!" he murmured, rasping her neck with his stubble. "Say my name when I'm inside you."

He drove into her in one merciless thrust, stretching and claiming without patience or gentleness, just raw, filthy need. She screamed his name.

Raking her nails down his back, she begged for more, faster and harder.

Was he proving a point? Fucking her as punishment for all those years apart? No. It was more than that. Every moan of pleasure was not just a debt repaid, but a pledge for the future. She met him thrust for thrust, hips rolling, teeth clashing until their bodies were slick with sweat.

"Look at me." Gripping her chin as her eyes fluttered shut, he spoke words torn from his soul. "You don't get to hide. Never again."

Meeting his fierce stare, she returned it with interest. "You're mine," she said, urging him on. "Fucking mine."

He brought her to the edge again, and they shattered

together, his name exploding from her lips as she clenched around him. They stayed locked together for the longest time, his forehead against hers, their breath mingling.

“Next time you decide to save my life, do it with me, or I swear to God, I’ll chain you to this bed and never let you go.”

“Promise?” she murmured, softening against him.

“Test me, sweetheart. Please…”

CHAPTER ELEVEN

They stayed under the shower for the longest time, steam curling around them like smoke from the battle they'd survived. There was a lot to make up for. Their bodies were still hungry, but her feelings for Elijah had deepened into a firm belief that he could and had changed. This made everything they were, and everything they felt and experienced, far deeper and more meaningful than before.

When he took her as if their lives depended on him filling her completely, she felt far more than physical satisfaction. A primal urge to be one with him in every way overwhelmed her. When she cried out his name, it was both a claim and an acceptance, a pledge more binding than marriage vows. He was hers, and she was his, and they would always belong together.

"Come while I'm deep inside you," he urged. "I need you to know there's no part of you I won't protect or cherish."

Once founded on sex and danger, their relationship had matured into something far deeper. As she claimed a riptide of release, she cried out, "I love you."

It was a while before she realized tears were streaming

down her face. Not tears of sorrow or pain, but love set free to express itself. They'd grown up believing love was something other people enjoyed, and that they didn't deserve it. Turns out they were wrong.

"What are you doing to me?"

She looked up as Elijah called out in the grip of release. It was the first time she could remember him losing control. He cursed fluently as he came inside her, but in shock rather than anger or regret.

Breathless and contented, they remained locked together, his chest heaving against her back. When he moved away, it was slow and careful, as if she were the most precious thing on earth.

"Are you trying to kill me with an overdose of pleasure?" Sable suggested when she finally released him and relaxed.

He laughed deep and slow. "I want you alive. Fit and back working on the team."

"Working." She sighed heavily. "Right now, that has to be a joke."

"The closest I'm ever likely to get to one," he conceded. "But that was great sex."

"Is that all it is for you?"

"Should it be more?" The words were out of his mouth before he could stop them.

She looked so hurt. Why did he keep doing that? Why were his shields always up? He reached out and pulled her close. "How many times must I prove I can't live without you? Losing you would be the greatest regret of my life."

Pushing back, she looked at him, her eyes full of tears.

"Crazy man. How long have you been holding that thought back?"

He shrugged. "Maybe for a moment, maybe since we met."

"You don't know?"

"Does it matter?"

This mix of emotion and need was new to him. Before Sable entered his life, if he wanted something, he took it. Now, if he wanted more, he had to give more, and keep on giving for the rest of his life. More than embracing that, he wanted it with every atom of his being.

"You're the only one who can break me," she husked, linking her arms around his neck. "You do know that?"

"I do now."

"I would never have left unless it was to save your life."

"I'm a big boy. I can look after myself."

"Big boy, yes," she conceded wryly. "Not sure about the rest."

Laughing, he gently disengaged her hands to kiss each fingertip in turn. His kisses were tender. Sex, though incredible, wasn't enough. He wanted more of Sable. He wanted all of her. Before her disappearance, he'd been a different man, but now he knew what he stood to lose.

"Hey," she breathed, "You okay? Still want me?"

So much, it was frightening. "I might even love you—just a little, of course."

Throwing her head back, she laughed with the confidence of a woman who knew she was loved. "I want all of you," she said fiercely.

"Me too," he admitted.

For once, that thought didn't alarm him.

~

Elijah cupped her face, his thumbs brushing away tears. "Look at me," he said quietly.

When she lifted her gaze to his, Elijah's eyes were stormy and unguarded. "You've changed me," he said, as if he could hardly believe it himself. "Something broke inside me when you left. I guess we never appreciate what we've got until it's too late."

Pressing his forehead to hers, he pledged softly, "I never want to be parted again—not for Black Meridian or to save my life. Not for anything on this earth while we're still breathing."

His words meant more than "I love you," but it was his smile—not cynical or mocking—that wiped the years away, allowing her to believe, perhaps for the first time, that this could work. "If I go missing, would you hunt me down?"

"To the ends of the earth and back. And then..." His expression shifted to pure teasing wickedness. "I'll fuck you until your legs won't carry you."

"Promise."

"You got it."

Beneath her laughter lay something deeper and more precious. She could feel Elijah's love warming and surrounding her, and she had never loved him more.

Yes.

Love.

Turned out they were both capable of loving and being loved. They just had to forget the past, concentrate on the here and now, and let that be their guide for the future.

Elijah's mouth brushed hers in a kiss that felt like a promise. "I love you," he said. "Get used to it."

Readily. Eagerly. She had no problem with that.

~

The sheets were rumpled and warm from their bodies when Sable woke from

the most peaceful night's sleep she could remember. When she moved, Elijah tightened his hold without opening his eyes. "Trying to sneak away?" he suggested, his voice still husky with sleep.

"There's work to do."

"The survivors are well cared for. I checked." He raised his cell. "We have to let the team feel useful."

"I guess. But it doesn't feel right to be idling here."

"Who said anything about idling?"

Rolling her beneath him, he caged her with his weight, his morning erection pressing against her belly. "Would you rather I pause to order coffee?"

"Don't you dare." She added something extremely rude about coffee.

"That's what I thought," he confirmed with a lazy grin.

Grinding slowly against her, he made sure she came straight away. "Greedy," he scolded, but with every touch, look, and each whispered word, it seemed he wanted to do more than deliver pleasure; he wanted to show how much he loved her.

"Would you have me any other way?"

He laughed. "I'd have you every way."

Proving it with a single thrust, drew a ragged moan of appreciation from her throat.

"Christ, Sable." His forehead dropped to hers as his hips kept rolling in deep, rhythmical strokes. "Will I ever get enough of you?"

"Hopefully not."

Things grew more upbeat after that. He made the headboard rattle and punched the air from her lungs, until the only sound was bodies colliding and her excited gasps. Clenching around him, she tested his control, but Elijah was ahead of her, shifting the angle and applying gentle, nudging pressure where she liked it.

"You taking advantage of me?"

"Who's taking advantage of who?" he demanded softly as she clenched his buttocks in a grip of iron. "It's time to let go—"

Before he could say "now," she did as he suggested.

"That's right, baby," he encouraged as she cried out in ecstasy with each successive wave.

Somehow, she came again. Back arching off the bed as the pleasure hit, her nails carving fresh lines down his back, she exclaimed with excited surprise and urged him on.

He kept going until she had extracted every last pulse of pleasure, then let go, pulsing hot inside her with a groan ripped from his soul.

They stayed together, joined, greedily drawing in air for a long time. "Still breathing?" he murmured as he swept damp hair from her brow.

"Barely," she admitted, gazing into his eyes.

He pressed a kiss to her mouth, then slanted a grin. "Good. Because I'm nowhere near done collecting interest on seven years—"

A soft chime rang through the stateroom, making them both smile. "Breakfast delivery," Elijah explained.

"Rain check?" she suggested. Without waiting for a reply, she slipped out of bed and went to freshen up.

Steam clouded the shower like a veil, while the faint clink of porcelain as the steward set up the breakfast table kept her thoughts grounded in reality. Danger was a given where Elijah was concerned. He would protect her, and as long as there was breath in her body, she would protect him.

Wrapping herself in a fluffy white robe, she called out,

"Coming, ready or not. Wow. That looks good." Her mouth watered as she stared at the plates laden with delicious treats. "I could eat everything on that table without any help from you."

"Sex gives me an appetite too," Elijah admitted with a wicked grin.

The smell of coffee, warm croissants, berries, and jam was irresistible. Elijah was too. He was looking at her with an expression she couldn't read. "Do you have to make it so hard to breathe?"

"I could say the same about you."

They stared at each other as morning light streamed through the floor-to-ceiling windows. His steward had opened these wide, allowing a light breeze to ruffle her hair.

This was their first meal in quite some time. It was made even more special by Sable. Had they ever been so relaxed? It felt almost normal. The future demanded vigilance, but they were used to that. Here and now, it was just the two of them and the peace he'd longed for and never found.

"So, the next few days," she began.

"Will be hectic as we get everyone settled."

"And then?"

"We keep moving. Avoid predictable patterns. Expect retaliation and prepare for it. No ports that broadcast our presence. No stops that leave us exposed."

"We remain at sea?"

"Not necessarily. Blood and Thunder owns a private island. You'll be welcome there," he added as Sable's eyes asked the question. He grazed her thumb in a grounding gesture. “When you’ve allowed me to, I’ve taken care of you. I always will.”

“I don’t need you to take care of me. I need you beside me.”

“I’m not going anywhere.” Closing his hand around hers, he brought her palm to his lips.

“Do you ever think there’s a world beyond this? A normal one?”

He let the question hang. “I think about it. More than I used to. But normal isn’t built for people like us.”

“But it could be,” she said, hope in her voice. “I like to think that somewhere, sometime, normal will be possible,”

“Coffee without danger,” he suggested as he poured them both a second cup.

“If you’re pouring, there is no danger.”

“Mornings that last longer than five minutes,” he suggested, glancing at his cell.

“Sun on a terrace without anyone watching,” she supplied with a grin.

“No one’s watching.” Leaning forward, he brushed her lips with his.

“Apart from a dozen cameras, monitored twenty-four seven in your control room.”

“Ah, those. You care?”

“No,” she admitted. “You?”

He let out a huff of laughter. “I’ve got bigger things to worry about. I want normality too, not just for a day. That’s what I want for us, even if it’s a fight every step of the way.”

“Does that mean no arguing about who makes the first strike on the next mission?”

“Tempting,” he said, his lips tugging with amusement. “Let’s compromise. You stab; I interrogate.”

“Compromise? Wow. You really have changed.” Her

laugh was low and real. “If you mess up, don’t expect a second chance.”

“Noted,” he said, grinning. “I’ll try not to die too quickly, then.”

When they were dressed and ready for the day, Sable was brushing out tangles in her hair when he came up behind her and slid his arms around her waist. Resting his chin on her head, he murmured, “Happy?”

“More than I can say.” Leaning into him, she whispered, “I love you. There, I’ve said it. I always have, and always will. It’s that simple, and that complicated.”

“I don’t know about complicated. I just know I’ve got the other half of me back.”

There was a lot to do, and they met only in passing. The rescued had been triaged and fed and were slowly coming around to the idea that safety was their new reality. There was even a gentle optimism aboard as the grand ramparts of the Grand Harbour came into view.

Thank goodness for that breakfast, Sable thought. Neither of them had a chance to eat for the rest of the day. By the time the *Seraphim* was back in her berth and all the survivors safely delivered to a hostel where they would be well cared for, she and Elijah had no energy to join a boisterous Blood and Thunder team supper and chose to retire to Elijah’s stateroom instead.

Standing on his private deck as the horizon bled rose and amber while day moved into night was a reminder that, even with so much evil in the world, they lived on a beautiful planet where good people would always outnumber the bad.

"I thought about throwing this into the sea many times," Elijah admitted, reaching for the ring around his neck.

"Same," Sable admitted, thinking of the raw amethyst she kept in her pocket as a talisman. "I meant to get rid of the amethyst you gave me, but I never could."

"Glad you kept it?"

"Very glad," she confessed.

"I'll keep my promise to have it polished and set. In the meantime, wear this. "May it always keep you safe."

She let out a soft exclamation as he slipped the chain he always wore around her neck, holding the gold ring that meant so much to him.

Digging in her pocket, she found the rough purple stone. "Take this in return as a keepsake from me." Rising on tiptoes, she looped her arms around his neck.

They kissed slow and deep. Elijah tasted of coffee and forever. "I love you," she whispered. Then she shouted, "I love you!" as if the ocean could record her words and keep them safe for all time.

"I'm home," Elijah said simply as he drew her back into his arms. Crushing her close as the sunset flared behind them, he pointed to the fiery sky. "Even Earth is celebrating our reunion. Shall we join the celestial celebrations?"

"It would be rude not to," she said.

CHAPTER TWELVE

They woke the next day in a tangle, her back to his chest. His hand lay curled over her heart, as if even in sleep he needed proof she was there. Blinking against the morning light slanting through half-open shutters, she began to roll out of bed.

"Stay," Elijah muttered, his voice gravelly with sleep. "I've got something for you—not that," he scolded softly. "This…"

Nothing could wake her faster than the sight of an amethyst, polished and gleaming in a platinum setting. "How did you manage that?" she asked, laughing in surprise. Her hand strayed to the gold chain at her neck. "We only exchanged these last night."

"Malta has some of the most remarkable jewelers, and I have some remarkable friends."

"You certainly do," she agreed, admiring the ring's brilliance and deep purple luster.

"Well? Are you going to put it on?"

"I want you to do it," she said. "Honestly, Elijah, I don't know what to say."

"Just say yes."

"To wearing your ring?"

"To becoming partners for life," he said, drawing her back into his arms. "Marry me. Make a half-decent man of me."

She pulled a teasing face. "Right now, I'd rather have the less-than-decent man, if that's all right with you. I want the downright filthy guy I love."

"How can I refuse when you ask so nicely?"

"You can't," she said.

The engines of the *Seraphim* thrummed beneath them, the vibration a gentle pressure against her naked body as she whispered, "Love you, Elijah. More than you know." Bringing the ring he'd given her to her lips, she kissed it. "You'll never get rid of me now."

Something raw crossed his face. "I can't believe you kept that amethyst all those years."

"Always." She reached for the chain at her neck. "Just as you kept this."

"Every morning for seven years, I woke and checked the chain," he said as Sable slipped the gold band on and off her finger. "I told myself that if the ring was still there, one day, you might walk back through the door. On other days, I told myself to throw it away and that I was better off without you."

"Were you?"

"I hated that you had that power over me."

"Not power. Love. But we didn't realize it then. I'm not sorry I left to save you when Black Meridian was trying to find and kill you. I wish I'd found a way to tell you what I planned to do."

"If you had, I'd have kept both of us safe."

"I couldn't take that chance. Not with your life." Sorry felt too small a word. She glanced at the ring on her finger, glowing like a promise.

"It may not be the perfect ring—"

"It's absolutely perfect," she insisted fiercely. "This stone has more history than any other piece of jewelry could hold."

He caught hold of her hand and stared into her eyes. "No more ghosts. If you walk away again, you take me with you."

"I'm not going anywhere. I'm home."

Swinging her into his arms, he carried her to the shower, where the warm stream of

water was like a benediction, washing away the pain of the past. Pulling her close, he buried his face in her neck. She felt the hammering of his heart against her ribs.

"I missed you so fucking much," he admitted. "I don't know how I kept breathing some days. Don't ever do that again."

She threaded her fingers through his hair, drawing back enough to meet his gaze. The storm had subsided in his eyes, replaced by something gentle and real.

And then he kissed her.

"Coffee now?" he suggested, wrapping her in a towel.

"If you promise to make this a daily ritual."

"Coffee or sex?"

"I'm sure we can reach a suitable arrangement."

"Deal, sweetheart." Elijah's slow, sexy smile heated her up from the inside out.

Mission complete, they left the *Seraphim* and returned to a safe house in Mdina, the Silent City, named for its deep, almost eerie quiet, especially after dark. A tiny population and traffic restrictions, coupled with loyal friends who would warn them of danger, made it the perfect sanctuary for two agents craving peace and privacy.

Sable had made the safe house comfortable and functional. Deep baths, relaxing sofas, cutting-edge tech, and every conceivable mod con made it the closest thing to home he'd ever known. "Making love with you is like coming home," she said, falling back on the pillows as if reading his mind.

"Making love with you is like running ten back-to-back marathons."

"Only ten?" she protested.

He waited until her breathing steadied, then slipped out of bed. A deep calm washed over him as he freshened up and dressed. Craving balmy air, he jogged down the stairs and stepped outside onto the narrow, cobbled street.

The night was warm, the area still. Everyone was asleep. After the violence of the mission, these rare moments of tranquility were almost unbearably precious. He pictured Sable deep in sleep, breathing softly. That in itself was a miracle, because she never relaxed. But tonight everything had reached the right conclusion for both of them, making the ending also a beginning.

Staring up at their open window, he smiled. The mission might be over, but for the first time in seven years, the future wasn't an empty horizon. They were together again, with a world of possibilities ahead.

~

She woke in a panic. Where was he?

Leaping out of bed, she stood at the arched window,

staring down at the empty street. The Silent City lived up to its name. No sound to be heard, just the low hush of night sliding like a phantom between the ancient walls.

It was beautiful, peaceful, terrifying. Silence was when her doubts screamed the loudest. Elijah had what he wanted, the vicious little voice inside her head insisted. Now he could sail away. You were just another loose end to tie off—

Then the heavy door opened.

His T-shirt clung to hard-muscled abs as he met her worried gaze. "I thought you'd weighed anchor without me," she admitted.

"I know what you thought. But I'm here to stay."

"You had plenty of time to learn to live without me."

"Enough to know I don't want to be without you."

Crossing the room, he stopped just short of touching her, close enough to feel his heat. "I'm done with half measures. Let's get married and create a dynasty."

She laughed at the crazy look of love on his face. "Can we start with a family?"

"I'll go with that." His lips slanted in the most attractive way. "Oh, and I've got something else for you. I couldn't resist…"

Her eyes widened as he flipped open the lid of a small velvet box.

"What the fuck is that?" she gasped.

"Apparently, it's a diamond engagement ring."

"So big it would light up the sky in a raid."

"So, I got you this too…" Reaching into his top pocket, he pulled out a simple platinum band.

"Gold and platinum. Two rings? You really are serious about this marriage thing."

"Never more so. Equal partners."

"Do I have to get down on one knee?"

"No. Your job is to stay by my side through gunfights and rescue missions, then cook when we get back."

"Equal partners? You learn to cook, or you go hungry."

Grabbing her, he kissed her sensitive neck until she begged for mercy.

The ring slid into place in a promise of forever. The end of one chapter, but the start of something new.

Crowding her back, hands planted either side of her head, Elijah promised, "I'm gonna spend the rest of my life making up for being cold and unfeeling, on the understanding that you sheathe your claws—at least while we're off-duty."

"No raking, gripping, or clinging allowed?"

"I wouldn't go that far." Rasping his stubble against her neck, he added in a tense whisper, "Don't leave me again. Never fucking again. Understood?"

"No fucking?" She feigned surprise. "Why, you promised me pleasure beyond imagining."

"You know what I mean," he growled against her mouth.

"I guess," she said as he lifted her.

They hit the mattress laughing hard enough to rattle the frame. Clothes weren't shed; they were ripped off. Parting her thighs with one powerful leg, Elijah drove into her in a single thrust, and she groaned his name like a prayer. "I'm yours," she gasped. "Always yours—"

Release tore through her without warning, vicious and bright, dragging his name from her throat in a broken scream. Elijah followed seconds later, burying himself to the hilt as he claimed relief with a raw, guttural sound.

Afterward, he held her close, rolling them until she was sprawled across his chest. Still joined, still pulsing, waves of pleasure went on and on, while their hearts beat in unison as if trying to occupy the same space.

Outside the window, Mdina slept beneath starlight older

than time, while Elijah traced the new rings on her finger. She felt his smile. “What?”

“Tomorrow, we sail again. I'm going to make the best of that voyage, by replaying tonight, one port at a time.”

“That sounds perfect to me.” She laughed softly against his skin. “Take me anywhere. Just never let me go.”

His arms tightened around her until her eyes grew heavy. “Forever,” he breathed as sleep claimed her.

EPILOGUE

The wedding

The *Seraphim* rode at anchor off a nameless cove on Gozo's western edge. In water so clear, the white sand beneath her keel glowed turquoise. No flags flew, no brass band played, no guests who weren't already crew or family forged in fire attended. Just the ship, the sea, and two people who had given their all for every inch of this moment.

Sable stood barefoot on the aft deck, the salt wind whipping the thin silk of her dress against her legs. The wedding gown she had chosen, a simple column design, was the color of twilight, the exact shade of the amethyst ring on her wedding finger. It had no back, just a few strategic straps. Elijah's eyes darkened the first time he saw it.

He waited at the rail for the ceremony to begin, his black linen shirt open at the neck, cuffs turned back to reveal a hint of fresh ink on his arm: Sable's initials, S.A.S., Sable Alexandrovna Steel. When she reached his side, they smiled into each other's eyes as if accepting that miracles could happen.

The celebrant who married them, a grizzled ex-mercenary with a voice like gravel, kept it brief. "Do you, Elijah, take this woman, knowing full well she's the most dangerous thing you'll ever hold in your arms?"

Elijah's answer was immediate. "Fuck yes."

Laughter rippled through the small crowd.

"And you, Sable: Do you take this man, knowing he'll hunt you down to the ends of the earth if you ever try to leave him again?"

She met Elijah's gaze steadily. "Try keeping me away from him."

The celebrant grunted approval. "Rings?"

Elijah produced two plain platinum bands, slid Sable's on first, then held out his hand. She took her time, tracing the new ink and old scars, before pushing Elijah's wedding ring home.

"By the power vested in me by the sea, common sense, and the fact that nobody here is stupid enough to argue with me, I pronounce you husband and wife. Kiss her before she changes her mind."

Elijah didn't waste time. Dragging her close, he kissed her as if his life depended on it, and she kissed him back just as fiercely, her fingers fisting in his shirt. When they broke apart, their guests erupted in cheers and whistles.

Leaving the crowd to enjoy a fabulous wedding feast, Elijah escorted her to their stateroom filled with displays of fragrant wedding flowers. "Wife," he murmured, tasting the word as if it were made of liquor and sin.

"Husband." She was already breathless as he carried her onto the balcony. The crew had strict instructions not to disturb them on pain of extremely creative consequences.

Eventually, he carried her back to bed, and they rang for food and drink.

"Shouldn't we rejoin our guests?" Sable asked, frowning.

"Do you know our guests? The Blood and Thunder team will keep everyone up all night celebrating. I doubt anyone will miss us."

When dawn broke, Sable snuggled against Elijah, content and happy.

He pulled her against his chest, brushed his lips against her throat, and murmured, "Good morning, wife. Welcome to the rest of your life."

"We have to get back in harness at some point," she pointed out.

"On our honeymoon?"

"A couple of days' break, then, if you insist," she murmured, softening into him.

"No more ghosts, Sable. No more running. We're home."

Smiling against his warm, naked body, she knew this was both family and home.

Four years later

The sea was a sheet of molten blue around Isla Celeste, home to the Blood and Thunder team. Only the most trusted partners and colleagues were allowed access, and it thrilled him to see Sable and their children on the private beach.

Barefoot in the shallows, dark hair glinting in the sun, she tried and failed to keep hold of two small whirlwinds racing around her—the twins. Their perfect chaos, as Sable called them, were three years old and already born conspirators. Shrieking with delight as they dodged their mother's grasp, they led Mara and Anna Marie in a merry dance while the two women did their best to help Sable contain them.

It became a game of lots of screaming and shouting,

dodging and giggling, as the twins raced around and the three women tried their hardest not to catch them.

It was a wonderful sight that made all they'd fought for worthwhile.

Their home was alive with laughter, tiny footsteps, and the quiet miracle of everyday moments. Children had changed them in ways no mission ever could. Fearless in the field, Sable had found an equally vital position on the team as chief of strategy. Her experience allowed her to plan and protect from a control room.

A natural home builder, she was a great mom to their kids, and he was reliably informed by his no-nonsense wife that patience and tenderness in dealing with children had softened his edges without dulling his fire.

She brought the twins to him, while Mara and Anna sat back on their sunbeds, chatting in the easy rhythm of people who had found peace.

Life couldn't get much better.

Mara and Anna had elected to stay with the team. Trusted and beloved guardians of the next generation, they had become integral to everything.

Farther up the beach came a chorus of familiar voices: Alexei's booming laugh, Dante arguing amiably with Diego, and Cesar and Conor locked in a good-natured contest involving Irish whiskey and terrible singing. The Blood and Thunder family reunited, not for a mission but for life.

Sable shaded her eyes and stared in the same direction. A smile lit her face, and for a heartbeat, he pictured every version of her: the woman who'd saved his life by walking away; the ruthless mercenary who risked everything to save those in need; the caring, strong-willed woman who followed a young girl's plight and stopped at nothing until she knew rescue was possible. Sable was a fighter in every way. She had returned to save lives with him, and he knew without doubt that she would fight like a tiger for her cubs.

That was true wealth.

The sand was warm beneath his feet and the sound of the sea folded around them as he slipped an arm around Sable's shoulders. She bent to lift one twin. He lifted the other, and they met in the middle in a group hug, laughter spilling from them as naturally as their next breath.

For years, he'd chased peace across oceans and battle-fields, never realizing it could feel so good. Like sunlight and laughter, or the scent of salt and jasmine, Sable's signature perfume, with her slender fingers laced through his, he had everything a man could ever need.

And his friends, he acknowledged, as their whoops of exuberance traveled across the beach. Blood and Thunder. Still standing. Still thriving. Still a family.

Taking all these blessings together, he was finally, finally, home.

COMING SOON

KANE - Book 5 in Susan's cowboy series, ACOSTAS RAW

Also, a brand-new series from Susan Stephens

Sign up for the newsletter so you don't miss the announcement.

Thank you for reading ELIJAH. If you can post a review, it would be wonderful. Thank You.

NEWSLETTER AND SOCIAL LINKS

Website https://www.susanstephens.net

Newsletter sign-up: https://dashboard.mailerlite.com/forms/888668/122749483237771112/share

Facebook https://www.facebook.com/susan.stephens.98499/

Facebook author page https://www.facebook.com/SusanStephensAuthor/

X https://x.com/susan_stephens?s=21&t=5oRPJ-7IHf1vatYxC0bcLQ

IG: https://www.instagram.com/susanstephens_author/

ABOUT THE AUTHOR

USA Today bestselling author Susan Stephens has sold more than 11 million books worldwide. Translated into 26 languages in 109 countries, Susan is best known for her emotionally charged contemporary romances, featuring powerful heroes, fearless heroines, and scorching chemistry.

ALSO BY SUSAN STEPHENS

ACOSTAS RAW

Cowboy Romance

1. BEAU
2. COLT
3. BLAKE
4. CASH
5. KANE – Coming Soon

BLOOD AND THUNDER

Romantic Suspense

1. ALEXEI
2. DANTE
3. DIEGO
4. CESAR
5. CONOR
6. ELIJAH

www.ingramcontent.com/pod-product-compliance
Lightning Source LLC
LaVergne TN
LVHW051013080826
845145LV00009B/2602

* 9 7 8 1 9 1 0 6 0 4 6 7 0 *